George Michael Edebohls

A Review of the History and Literature of Appendicitis

George Michael Edebohls

A Review of the History and Literature of Appendicitis

ISBN/EAN: 9783742860804

Manufactured in Europe, USA, Canada, Australia, Japa

Cover: Foto ©Andreas Hilbeck / pixelio.de

Manufactured and distributed by brebook publishing software
(www.brebook.com)

George Michael Edebohls

A Review of the History and Literature of Appendicitis

A Review of the History and Literature of Appendicitis

BY

GEORGE M. EDEBOHLS, A.M., M.D.

NEW YORK

Reprint from the MEDICAL RECORD, *November 25, 1899*

NEW YORK:

THE PUBLISHERS' PRINTING COMPANY

32, 34 LAFAYETTE PLACE

1899

A REVIEW OF THE HISTORY AND LITERATURE OF APPENDICITIS.

By GEORGE M. EDEBOHLS, A.M., M.D.,

NEW YORK.

DURING the early part of the present year the writer had occasion to look up one or two points in connection with the subject of appendicitis. He became interested and more and more deeply involved in the literature, until after a number of months, during which all his spare moments were devoted to the task, he found that he had read and passed in review about all that has ever been written upon appendicitis. The magnitude of the labor becomes apparent when it is stated that the literature of appendicitis, up to and inclusive of the year 1898, embraces more than twenty-five hundred journal articles, dissertations, and books, all but a very small fractional part of which the writer has consulted in the original. As illustrating the rapid growth of the literature it may be stated that more than one-half of the twenty-five hundred journal articles, dissertations, and books have appeared within the past five years.

Upon the conclusion of the task, and at the suggestion of the editor of the MEDICAL RECORD, who thought that a historical review of the subject of appendicitis might interest some of the readers of his journal, the following notes were arranged for publication.

Nomenclature.—Epityphlitis, ecphyaditis, and scolecoiditis have been proposed by Kuester, Morris, and Gerster, respectively, as synonyms for appendicitis. The term appendicitis, however, though a barbarism, is too firmly established by long and universal usage, both among the profession and the laity, to be displaced at this late day. We bow to the inevitable, and, for reasons which have been well set forth by Ellis,[109] accept the term appendicitis.

General Historical Data.—The early history of appendicitis is merged with and emerges from that of iliac phlegmon, typhlitis, paratyphlitis, and perityphlitis. Saracenus, in a letter dated August 28, 1642, published by Roussel,[304] describes an abscess in the right iliac region with discharge of fecal matter and fourteen lumbricoid worms, possibly the most ancient clear case of perityphlitic or appendicular abscess on record. A number of similar cases were published during more than a hundred years following, before Mestivier,[232] in 1759, recognized appendicitis as a distinct entity. Mestivier incised an abscess in the right groin, in a woman far advanced in pregnancy, and on autopsy found at the bottom of the abscess the appendix vermiformis perforated by a pin. Toward the end of the eighteenth and during the early half of the nineteeth century, appendicitis with perforation and abscess formation was often found in the dead-house and described by numerous writers. Yet, as late as 1838, so learned a man as Albers,[7] writing at length on typhlitis and perityphlitis, does not even mention the appendix— proof that a knowledge of the existence of appendicitis was by no means general at that time. The complications and sequelæ of appendicitis, especially those fatal in character, were also noted during the early half of the present century. In 1846 Landsberg[191] reported two cases of hernia, one inguinal and one femoral, containing the appendix. Hall,[143] Zdekauer,[375] Monks,[240] Ohlmacher,[208] Pollosson,[277] Rotter,[303] Routier,[303] Kayser,[174] Ginnard,[140] and Gross[138] have since reported like experiences. In 1847 the diagnosis of appendicitis began to be made during life by Cless,[61] Hancock,[140] and others. In the fifties Cless,[62] Bamberger,[19] and Leudet[201] reported large numbers of personal observations of perforative appendicitis with autopsies; Leudet, for example, reporting thirteen cases of perforation and seventeen cases of simple ulceration of the appendix observed by him in three years. Skoda,[321] in 1862, noted the spontaneous cure of appendicitis by obliteration, and advises a "hardening process" treatment with that end in view. With,[307] in 1879, fully described peritonitis appendicularis, and Bierhoff,[34] in 1880, gave an excellent, full, and elaborate description of the pathology of appendicitis, modern in every respect except as to bacteriology. The classic of Fitz,[116] which appeared in 1886, may fairly be said to have given the impetus to the intense and practical study of appendicitis of latter years.

The bacteriology of appendicitis first received attention in 1891, chiefly at the hands of the Frenchmen Adenot[5] and Gouillioud,[138] soon followed by Eckehorn,[106] Weir,[300] Robb,[293] Hodenpyl,[161] and others.

The diagnosis of acute appendicitis was advanced more than by all previous knowledge combined, by McBurney,[219] when, in 1889, he discovered and established the value of "McBurney's point." The introduction and elaboration, in 1894, by Edebohls,[96] of palpation of the vermiform appendix finally placed us in a position to diagnose clearly and positively every case of chronic, and nearly every case of acute, appendicitis.

The history of the origin and development of the operative treatment of perityphlitic abscess and of appendicitis will receive full attention later on under a special heading.

Frequency of Appendicitis.—As regards both the frequency of appendicitis and its relative frequency in the two sexes, the most remarkable and apparently irreconcilable statements are made by various investigators. While the belief is current that appendicitis affects males in larger proportion than females, Einhorn,[105] in eighteen thousand successive autopsies, found perforating appendicitis in 0.55 per cent. of males and 0.57 per cent. of females, and Robinson[294] in one hundred and twenty-eight autopsies as they came found evidences of past peritonitis on and about the appendix in sixty-six per cent. of female and fifty-six per cent. of male bodies.

With[367] quotes Toft as finding in three hundred autopsies one hundred and ninety entirely normal appendices and one hundred and ten appendices presenting more or less evidences of disease. Wallis,[356] on the contrary, in autopsies extending over nearly five years found only 1.7 per cent. of all appendices presenting evidences of disease. Fitz,[110] in 1886, reports two hundred and fifty-seven cases of perforative appendicitis observed by him post mortem, and comments upon the frequency with which autopsy shows long-standing chronic inflammation without acute attacks. Ribbert[267] and Zuckerkandl[376] have given us post-mortem statistics of obliterating appendicitis. The former, in four hundred autopsies, found the appendix partially obliterated in 21.5 per cent. and completely obliterated in 3.5 per cent.; the latter, in two hundred and thirty-two examinations, found 9.9 per cent. of partial and 13.8 per cent. of complete inflammatory obliteration of the lumen of the appendix. Clinically, Edebohls[101] finds that four per cent. of all women have appendicitis.

Anatomy of the Vermiform Appendix.—According to Kelynack,[177] the existence of the appendix does not appear to have been recognized previous to the sixteenth century, when it was described by Carpi, Estienne, and Vidus Vidius, the latter of whom applied the qualifying term "vermiform." Santorini and Sabatier described it quite satisfactorily in the seventeenth century. But it is only since the appearance of the classic of Lieberkühn,[209] in 1739, and that of Vosse,[355] in 1749, that a description of the vermiform appendix has found its way into every text-book of anatomy.

Finnell,[116] in 1869, measured fifty male and fifty female appendices, and found the appendix averaged one-half inch longer in women than in men. Mott,[249] Biggs,[35] Dade,[73] and others have put on record exceptionally long appendices. The general anatomy of the appendix has received consideration at the hands of Hewson,[154] Ribbert,[287] and many others. Ribbert's macro- and microscopical examinations of four hundred appendices deserve special mention. The variations of position observed post mortem have been minutely investigated by Bryant.[50] The peritoneal folds and fossæ in the immediate neighborhood of the appendix are fully described and pictured by Lockwood and Rolleston,[209] Kelynack,[177] and Jonnesco.[169] Swan[339] records the only well-authenticated case of congenital absence of the appendix.

Etiology of Appendicitis.—The causative factors in the production of appendicitis are universally admitted by all writers to be very generally local in character. Fox,[125] in 1885, called attention to the analogy between quinsy and appendicitis, in both of which lymphoid tissues identical in structure were involved. Atkinson[12] and Bloomfield,[39] in 1895, discussed heredity as a cause, and "family appendicitis" was again brought forward by Faisans[111] in 1896. In 1891 Adenot[5] and Gouillioud[136] developed the important rôle played by bacteria in the etiology of appendicitis. In 1895 and 1896 quite a crop of general causes of appendicitis sprang up in the literature. Frazer[126] writes of uratic typhlitis, Matthieu[216] of *la lithiase appendiculaire*, and Simons[323] describes a case of gouty appendicitis. Rheumatism was advanced as a cause by Sutherland,[337] followed by Beverley Robinson.[295] Byron Robinson[294] finds the chief exciting cause of appendicitis in the action of the psoas muscle. La grippe is considered by a number of New York physicians of prominence and large experience a frequent cause of attacks of appendicitis. The etiology of relapses has been carefully and minutely studied by von Mayer.[349] Goluboff[135] calls appendicitis an epidemic infectious disease. Edebohls[100] has pointed out the rôle played by movable right kidney in the production of appendicitis.

Pathology of Appendicitis.—The general gross pathology of appendicitis has received full attention in the writings of Leudet,[201] With,[407] Bierhof,[34] Porter,[281] Fitz,[116] and numerous others. The microscopical appearances have been carefully studied by Craig,[67] Ribbert,[287] Letulle and Weinberg.[200] The spontaneous cure of appendicitis by obliteration was noted by Skoda[334] in 1862. and the cure of perforation of the appendix by the same process was recorded by Pepper[266] in 1867. Later, Senn,[315] Zuckerkandl,[410] and Piersol[270] wrote on "appendicitis obliterans," the last-named author designating it nature's cure. Catarrhal appendicitis, though generally recognized, has received but scant description, the only noteworthy contribution, perhaps, being that of Deaver.[79] The pathology of interval cases is well described and pictured by Abbe.[1] "Appendicite sous-hépatique" is considered worthy of special description by Glantenay.[133] The homology of appendicitis with salpingitis is insisted upon by Delbet.[84] A solitary case of intramural abscess of the appendix is recorded by Pilliet,[273] and a solitary observation of suppurative typhlitis with a normal appendix by Lop.[212]

Foreign Bodies in the Appendix.—In former years foreign bodies in the appendix were considered under the head of etiology of appendicitis. In the light of modern views the permanent lodgment of foreign bodies in the appendix is probably more frequently the result than the cause of appendicitis. In the following list, by no means complete, of foreign bodies found in the appendix, reference to publication is omitted.

Entozoa have been found in the appendix in the

following varieties: Ascarides lumbricoides (Becquerel, Patterson, Lang, Buck, Cuthbertson); Oxyuris vermicularis (Bierhof); Tricocephalus dispar (Bierhof).

Coproliths have been found by everybody who has had much to do with post-mortem investigations or with the surgery of the appendix. Next to coproliths, pins have been the foreign bodies most frequently met in the appendix (Mestivier, Hewitt, Joffroy, Legg, Boussi, Ashby, Shoemaker, McPhaedran, Calmer, Vanderveer, Park).

Other foreign bodies found in the appendix are: grape seeds (Briske, Pepper, Noyes, Hebb); melon seeds (Tavignot, Malespine, Edebohls); a chocolate nut (Prescott); a grain of oat (Price, Howe); cherry stones (Theurer, Werner, Reignier, Ferguson, Formad); raspberry seeds (Vedder, Craig); prune stones (Vidal, Stuetzle); a date seed (Leaman); orange seeds (Thornton, Service); a bean (Cliquet, Haeker, Wyman); tomato seeds (Edebohls); a fruit stone (Firket); huckleberry seeds (Brundage); blackberry seeds (Vanderveer, Wilson); shell of hazelnut (Southam); a piece of chestnut (Owens, Formad); peanuts (Rosenheimer); hair (Peterson, Hildebrandt); a bristle (Ward, Gibbons, Ulloa y Geralt); a glazier's point of zinc (Bartlett); a globule of solder (Morton); a gelatin capsule (Roberts); a piece of bone (Ferguson, Coleman); a piece of screw nail (Ferguson); a rifle cartridge (Ransohoff); fin of a fish (Ashton); knot of a heavy silk ligature from a tubo-ovarian pedicle (Edebohls).

Pathological Conditions Other than Inflammation Affecting the Vermiform Appendix.—For the sake of completeness I append a list of various diseased conditions of the appendix other than inflammatory, which I have found recorded in the literature: Prolapse of mucous membrane of appendix (Rolleston[300]); invagination of appendix (McKidd[228]); intussusception of the appendix (McGraw,[226] Wright and Renshaw,[371] Waterhouse[357]); cystic dilatation of appendix (Gruber,[139] Shoemaker,[321] Hawkins,[161] Coats[63]); retention cyst of appendix (Maylard,[217] Sonnenburg[329]); mucocele of appendix (Féré,[114] Vimont,[348] Baillet[16]); hydrops of vermiform appendix (Combemarle,[65] Guttmann,[141] Ribbert[287]); tuberculosis of appendix (Apert[10] and numerous others); echinococcus of appendix (Bierhof,[33] Birch-Hirschfeld[37]); actinomycosis of appendix (Ekehorn,[100] Gangolph and Duplant,[129] Czerny[72]); cystic degeneration or alveolar carcinoma of appendix (Rokitansky[229]); primary colloid cancer of appendix (Draper[90]); primary cancer of appendix (Mosse and Daunic[247]); cancer of appendix (Stimson[336]); primary adenocarcinoma of appendix (Wright[372]); primary endothelial sarcomata of appendix (Glazebrook[134]).

Bacteriology of the Appendix.—Clarke[67] has felicitously entitled the appendix a culture tube. Since Adenot[5] and Gouillioud,[130] in 1891, began the study of the bacteriology of the appendix and showed appendicitis to be due, in practically every case, to bacterial invasion of the appendix walls, most frequently by the bacterium coli commune, researches in this direction have been continued with uninterrupted zeal and enthusiasm by a number of workers. Ekehorn,[100] in 1892, proved that the bacterium coli manifested diferent degrees of virulence in different cases, and that it is present in every form of appendicitis, from the catarrhal onward. Robb,[293] in 1892, reported a case of associated streptococcus infection of the vermiform appendix and right Fallopian tube. Morris,[239] in 1893, published the first article with the distinct title, "Infectious Appendicitis." Weir,[360] in 1893, found the diplococcus pneumoniæ in nearly pure culture in the appendix in a case of purulent appendicitis, and Ohlmacher,[259] in the same year, found the proteus vulgaris. Hodenpyl,[157] in 1893, contributed a most important bacteriological study of appendicitis based upon an examination of thirty-five cases. Achard and Broca,[4] in 1897, presented a noteworthy résumé of the bacteria found in the peritoneal exudate in twenty cases of appendicitis. Beaussenat[26] has given us the most important paper on experimental appendicitis. His experiments, supplemented by those of Josué,[171] prove that germs may invade the ·lymphoid tissue of the appendix by way of the blood and by way of the lymphatics, as well as through the mucous membrane. Hartmann and Reymond[150] report an observation of the passage of the bacterium coli from an appendix abscess through the intact bladder wall, causing infectious cystitis.

Complications of Appendicitis.—The complications of appendicitis are impressive by reason of both their number and their gravity. Mortier,[241] Little,[208] Sheffey,[318] Bennett,[28] Lincoln,[206] Perry,[208] Andrews,[9] Pitres,[275] Hendricks,[153] Englisch,[110] Dale,[74] Bierhof,[33] Murray,[253] Weiss,[362] and Morris[240] have recorded cases of intestinal strangulation, the result of appendicitis. Death from hemorrhage has resulted from perforative ulceration, due to appendicitis, (*a*) of the small intestine (Osler[260]); (*b*) of the sigmoid (Stedman[333]); (*c*) of the right external iliac artery (Powell,[283] Sourdille[331]); (*d*) of the right iliac vein (Fowler,[120] Lewis[204]).

Other complications or sequelæ noted are: Prolapse of the mucous membrane of the appendix into the cæcum (Rolleston[300]); invagination of the appendix (McKidd[228]); discharge of the gangrenous appendix per rectum (Jackson,[164] Long[210]); fæcal fistula (Long,[211] Rioblanc,[292] and numerous others); appendiculo-intestinal fistula through a suppurating mesenteric gland (Packard[261]); vesico-intestinal fistula (Keen[175]); perforation of the colon, rectum, and bladder (Rochester[297]); perforation of the bladder (Clark,[50] Boardman,[40] Cameron[53]); perforation into the bladder with formation of stone (Fowler[124]); localized and general peritonitis, by almost every writer; obliteration of the right crural artery by arteritis (Bérard[29]); embolism of the left anterior tibial artery, with gangrene of the leg (Scheibenzuber[319]); embolism of the pulmonary artery (McGregor); phlebitis of the right iliac; phlebitis of the left leg (Freeman[127]); thrombosis of the right femoral vein (Legg[194]); phlebitis and thrombosis of the vena mesenterica magna and portal pylephlebitis (Aufrecht,[11] Ssawostjun w[332]); purulent inflammation of the portal vein (Baernhoff,[15] Moers,[335] Machell,[214] Mynter,[254] Carless[54]); portal pylephlebitis and hepatic abscess (Traube,[345] Pierson,[271] Davat,[75] Boussi,[42] Jorand[179]); hepatic abscess, "la foie appendiculaire" of Dieulafoy[88] (Krakowitzer,[183] Ashby,[12] De Gennes,[82] Shoemaker,[321] Harte,[148] Achard,[4] Nuding,[258] Pilliet and Costes,[272] Sheen,[317] Morton[242]); left perinephritic abscess, perforation of the diaphragm, left purulent pleuritis (Coats[63]); right perinephritic abscess, perforation of the diaphragm, right empyema (Ardouard,[11] Shiels,[319] Rioblanc[292]); the same, with perforation of the lung (Thacher[343]); the same, with gangrene of the lung (Mader[216]); right pleuro-pneumonia (Dupré[92]); subphrenic abscess (Sachs,[307] Freiberg[128]); perforation of the eighth intercostal space and right lung (McCallum,[224] McPhaedran[229]); purulent cystitis, due to migration of the bacterium coli commune through the intact bladder wall (Hartmann and Reymond[150]); prevesical abscess (Tuffier[347]); ureteritis, pyelonephritis (Hectoen[152]); scrotal abscess and purulent pleuritis (Lemailey[197]); multiple distant abscesses (Pirard[247]); glycosuria (Leidy[196]); fusion of the appendix to the gall bladder (Czerny,[72] Edebohls). Beurnier,[30] Czerny,[72] and Shoemaker[320] have devoted special attention to the coexistence of appendicitis and membranous colitis.

Herniæ Containing the Appendix.—The appendix has frequently been found among the contents of a hernial sac. Landsberg,[295] Hall,[143] Zdekauer,[375] Monks,[230] Ohlmacher,[259] Kayser,[174] and Gross[136] have recorded cases of inguinal hernia containing the appendix. The case of Hall is historical from the fact that it represents the first removal of the appendix with survival of the patient. Landsberg,[191] Pollosson,[277] Rotter,[303] Routier,[305] Ginnard,[140] and Vanderveer[347 bis] have found the appendix as part of the contents of a femoral hernia.

Appendicitis Associated with Diseased Conditions of the Pelvic Organs.—The association of an inflamed appendix with every variety of diseased conditions of the pelvic organs, more especially of women, is a matter of almost daily observation in the practice of abdominal surgery. In some cases the appendix is the starting-point of the diseased action, in others it becomes involved secondarily to disease affecting primarily the pelvic viscera. Baldy,[17] Richelot,[291] Mixter[234], Robb,[293] Jaggard,[165] Binckley,[38] McGuire,[227] and Deaver[81] have, among others, given special attention in their writings to this aspect of our subject.

Appendicitis Complicating Pregnancy, Labor, and the Puerperal State.—The classical case of Mestivier,[232] the first in which a diseased appendix, in this case containing a pin, was recognized at autopsy as the cause of an abscess in the right iliac fossa, occurred in a woman eight months pregnant. The case of Hancock,[146] no less historical as representing the first successful operation for deep-seated perityphlitic abscess, also occurred in a woman eight months pregnant. The patient miscarried four days after operation. The next case recorded is that of Porcher,[260] whose patient miscarried at five months, died suddenly and unexpectedly fourteen hours afterward, and was found on post-mortem to have purulent appendicitis and peritonitis. Hirst,[156] in 1890, operated upon a woman six months pregnant for supposed acute suppurative appendicitis. He found chronic appendicitis with a few adhesions. The patient died two days after the operation; there was no autopsy. Mixter,[734] in 1891, reports a case of appendicitis originating in the seventh month of pregnancy; successful operation was performed two months after the termination of pregnancy. Wiggin,[364] in 1892, reports an autopsy upon a woman three months pregnant, who died as the result of perforative appendicitis. Petersen,[269] in 1893, records a case of appendicitis on the seventh day following a labor at term, with rupture of the abscess into the bowel and recovery without operation. Krafft[192] reports a successful operation for purulent appendicitis, performed January 29, 1893, upon a woman aged twenty-five years, four and a half months advanced in pregnancy. The patient had double pleuritis and acute endocarditis immediately preceding the appendicitis. The pregnancy proceeded to term without interruption, and terminated in the birth of a boy whom the mother, in memory of her experience, christened Malgrétout. Grandin,[137] in 1893, reports a case of acute catarrhal appendicitis six days after delivery at term; recovery without operation. Also a case of miscarriage at three months complicated with acute catarrhal appendicitis. Mundé,[250] in 1894, reports the successful evacuation of a peri-appendicular abscess in a woman eight months pregnant. A dead child was born one week after operation.

From this time onward reports of cases of appendicitis occurring in pregnant women become more numerous. Hind,[155] in 1895, reports a case having medicolegal bearings. A woman, pregnant near term, was violently assaulted. Labor set in, and death followed two days after delivery. Autopsy showed an abscess due to perforation of the appendix. Bayley,[25] in the same year, records an attack of appendicitis during the sixth month of pregnancy; recovery took place without operation, followed by delivery at term. McArthur,[218] also in 1895, reports two operations for acute appendicitis in pregnant women, both fatal. Johnson,[169] in 1896, reports a successful operation for non-suppurative appendicitis in a woman three and a half months pregnant, followed by confinement at term. Robson,[298] in the same year, records a successful operation for appendicitis thirty-six hours after accouchement at the eighth month. McCosh,[225] in 1897, reports a successful operation for appendicitis during the sixth month of pregnancy, with subsequent delivery at term. Abrahams,[2] in 1897, collected the more recent cases of appendicitis during pregnancy from the literature, giving cases of his own together with additional cases of Mundé, Harrison, Thomason, Crutcher, and Hirst. For details of these the reader is referred to the descriptions and abstracts of Abrahams. Deaver,[81] in 1898, wrote a valuable paper on appendicitis in relation to disease of the uterine adnexa and pregnancy. Finally Gerster,[131] in 1899, contributes three personal observations of appendicitis successfully operated upon during the eighth, second, and fifth months, respectively, of pregnancy, with premature labor in the first and delivery at term in the second and third cases.

The Diagnosis of Appendicitis.—The symptoms and signs of perityphlitic abscess, especially in the later stages of the disease, have been pretty clearly understood by the profession ever since the time of Mestivier. Beginning with 1847, the diagnosis of perforation of the appendix, or of its involvement in the inflammatory process, began to be made more frequently, among the first by Cless[61] and Hancock.[146] Gibney,[132] in 1881, wrote a very creditable paper on the differential diagnosis between appendicitis and hip-joint disease. Valuable modern contributions have been presented by Morton,[245] Deaver,[78] Meek,[230] Fowler,[122] Murphy,[251] and numerous others. Fowler[122] has gone very fully into the differential diagnosis of appendicitis in the female.

The greatest advance in the diagnosis of acute appendicitis we owe to the keen observations of McBurney,[219] which, in 1889, gave us that valuable aid in diagnosis now known the world over as "the McBurney point." Rosenthal[301] makes a weak priority claim for Traube in relation to the discovery of the point.

The elaboration and publication by Edebohls,[96] in 1894, of his method of palpation of the vermiform appendix finally made those who have become conversant with the method masters of the situation as regards the diagnosis of both acute and chronic appendicitis. It is true a thickened, inflamed appendix had previously now and then been felt through the abdominal walls. Treves,[346] in 1889, and Cameron,[53] in 1893, each reported such an experience, and Duncan,[91] in 1892, says that the position of an inflamed appendix may often be felt. The positive determination of the health or otherwise of the appendix, however, by direct examination and palpation of the organ in each and every case presenting, was considered an impossibility and never attempted previous to the publication of Edebohls.

Among those who have adopted Edebohls' method of palpation of the appendix, and who depend upon it for the diagnosis of appendicitis, may be mentioned Deaver,[78] Long,[211] Halsted,[146] Shrady,[322] Morris,[240] Noble,[256] Mynter,[254] Murphy, Beck,[27] and Kelly.[178]

The Medical Treatment of Appendicitis.—Volumes have been written upon the medical and surgical treatment of appendicitis. The history of the origin and development of the surgical treatment of the affection will receive attention presently. The medical treatment has received full consideration at the hands of all the older and many of the more recent clinicians, and the principles supposed to underlie it are well known to every practitioner. Few physicians advocate, with With,[307] medical treatment only for all cases. A large number of prominent internists, with Eliot,[107] Fitz,[116] and others, consider appendicitis essentially a surgical affection. As long ago as 1848, Smith[325] expressed doubt as to the efficacy of all local applications, including leeches, saying of the latter: "If you are going to use leeches in typhlitis apply them at the anus, not over the swelling." The only recommendation of electricity in the treatment of appendicitis is by Williams.[305]

The Surgical Treatment of Appendicitis.—The earliest recorded case of operation for appendicitis is generally credited to Mestivier,[232] who, in 1759, incised and drained an abscess in the right inguinal region. The patient died, and the autopsy disclosed an appendix perforated by a pin. A few operations for so-called perityphlitic abscess which had slowly perforated the abdominal parietes and become, in part at least, subcutaneous, were reported between 1759 and 1848. Dupuytren[93] operated thus in 1815 and 1828; Ahrt[6] in 1832, and Parker[262] in 1843. In all of these cases fluctuation was distinctly made out, and pus was encountered in the subcutaneous tissues of the abdominal wall.

Hancock,[146] on April 17, 1848, performed the first deliberate operation for deep-seated suppuration of appendicular origin. He operated on the fifteenth day of illness, and before fluctuation became apparent, reaching the pus collection by a four-inch incision extending from just above the right anterior superior spine of the ilium downward and inward along Poupart's ligament. His patient recovered. On the strength of this case Hancock proposed to operate early in these cases before fluctuation appeared, remarking that patients do not usually live to fluctuation. His teaching, however, found no echo in medical literature until reiterated by Lewis[203] in 1856. His example was first imitated after eighteen years by Parker,[262] the publication of whose case, in 1867, may fairly be said to have directly inaugurated the modern surgical treatment of abscesses of appendicular origin, and indirectly to have led to the modern surgery of the appendix.

By many writers Parker is credited with the first operation for perityphlitic abscess in 1843. Parker, in 1867, reported four cases of perityphlitic abscess operated upon, the first operation being performed in 1843. In his first three cases, however, subcutaneous fluctuation or phlegmon invited the incision, as it had done in the cases already cited as previously reported. Parker's first operation for deep-seated suppuration, prior to fluctuation, was performed in 1866, nearly eighteen years after the original operation of Hancock. His patient also recovered.

From 1867 to 1884 the initiative taken by Hancock and Parker in opening and draining so-called perityphlitic abscesses before fluctuation was evident was enthusiastically taken up and followed, especially by American surgeons, New York being at first the chief focus of the new surgical activity. Buck, Sands, Weber, Bontecou, Burge, Whitall, Ward, Kelsey, Holden, Clarke, Ely, Raub, Bacon, Clay, North, Beach, Chamberlain, Koehler, Mynter, Weir, Byrd, Pierson, were among the earliest performers or reporters of operations for the evacuation of deeply seated abscesses of appendicular origin. Noyes,[267] in 1883, collected the reports of one hundred operations for perityphlitic abscess.

Nearly all of the perityphlitic abscesses operated upon during this period were opened by the original classical incision of Hancock. Weber[358] at first contented himself with incising down to, but not through, the fascia transversalis, and this method was even advocated as the routine procedure by Whitall.[363] Kolb,[190] in 1860, practised puncture of the abscess by the trocar and dilatation of the opening with sponge tents. Muenchmeyer,[219] in 1860, was the first to practise a counter-opening in the loin to obtain better drainage, a procedure which has since found many imitators. Buck,[43] in 1861, evacuated a pelvic abscess, presumably of appendicular origin, by puncture through the rectum. Bartholow,[19] in 1866, credits Buck with approaching a perityphlitic abscess from beneath Poupart's ligament by an incision carried through the fascia lata of the right thigh, thence working his way upward beneath Poupart's ligament to the abdomen. I have been unable to find the original account by Buck of this procedure. Barlow and Godlee,[20] in 1885, operated upon a case of appendicular abscess by two incisions, one median, exploratory in character, and one lateral, over the abscess, to evacuate the pus. This procedure has been followed in a number of cases by various operators. Kroenlein,[185] in 1887, reported the first case of operation for perityphlitic abscess under Listerism. Homans,[159] in 1886, took a decided step in advance in the case of an appendicular abscess deeply situated against the posterior abdominal wall. He opened the abdomen through the usual incision above and parallel to Poupart's ligament, and evacuated the abscess across the free peritoneal cavity while protecting the latter against infection by suitably placed packing. This has become and remained standard modern practice. Not so the procedure of Edebohls,[95] who in 1889, in a similar case, closed the peritoneum by suture, dissected it up, and opened the abscess retroperitoneally. Byrd,[52] in 1881, in a case of perforative appendicitis with two additional ulcerative perforations of the cæcum, adopted the procedure, nothing less than brilliant for that day, of converting the three openings into one large one, establishing an artificial anus by stitching the bowel opening to the wound, and irrigating and draining the free peritoneal cavity. His patient recovered. Mention should, finally, be made of Kottmann's[181] plan of opening the abscess by Vienna paste, the only advocacy or practice of this method which I have found recorded in the literature.

The above data all refer to operations for the evacuation of perityphlitic abscesses of appendicular origin undertaken before the time at which operations upon the appendix itself came into vogue. The history of the surgery of the appendix itself, and data in connection therewith, will presently receive attention. Before proceeding to this chapter of the history of appendicitis, however, two subjects, that of aspiration, exploratory or curative, of perityphlitic abscesses, and that of so-called left-sided appendicitis, deserve a moment's consideration.

Exploratory Puncture.—Bontecou,[41] in 1873, reported two cases of operation for perityphlitic abscess in which he employed previous aspiration to determine the presence of pus. Prior to that time we find recorded, now and then, a crude attempt to establish the presence of pus by an oblique puncture with a narrow knife, a grooved needle, or a trocar. Potter,[262] in 1879, reported a cure of perityphlitic abscess following a single aspiration of the contained pus. Peltzer,[265] in 1882, observed a cure following two aspirations of the pus, followed each time by irrigation of the abscess cavity with a solution of salicylic acid. Bull,[46] in 1886, advocates dropping all time limits and operating as soon as pus can be discovered by the needle. At about this period exploratory punctures for diagnostic purposes were much in vogue. Gradually, however, they yielded place to the increasing positiveness with which diagnosis could be reached without their aid, until at the present day probably no surgeon of any prominence either employs or recommends the needle for diagnosis.

Left-Sided Appendicitis.—As regards left-sided appendicitis the only genuine case thereof on record is that of Biegi,[31] which occurred in a soldier who died of appendicitis and was found on autopsy to have a complete transposition of all the viscera. The case of Bontecou,[41] in which death resulted from ulcerative perforation of the small intestine into the left iliac fossa; that of Traube,[346] of a perityphlitic abscess pointing on the left side; and the three cases reported by Fowler,[119] in which the cæcum and appendix were displaced to the left, all originated primarily in the right iliac fossa. So did the case of Coats,[63] in which empyema of the left chest followed perforation of the diaphragm by pus from an abscess of appendicular origin.

Surgery of the Appendix.—We have finished with the history of the era when operations for the evacuation and drainage of perityphlitic abscesses constituted, with the few exceptions mentioned, the sole surgical resource in the treatment of appendicitis, or rather of its results. We come now to the period which saw the birth of the surgery proper of the appendix itself. We will consider the surgery of the appendix as applied, first, to the treatment of acute appendicitis, and, secondly, to the treatment of chronic, relapsing, and interval cases.

The first recorded operation upon the appendix itself was planned by Dr. Mahomed and executed on August 24, 1883, by Symonds.[340] Mahomed diagnosticated a stone in the appendix. Symonds removed the stone, three-fourths by one-half inch in size, through the ordinary incision for tying the external iliac artery, approaching the appendix from behind, through peritoneal adhesions, opening the appendix, extracting the stone, and closing the opening in the appendix by Lembert sutures. The patient recovered and was cured of all his symptoms. In connection with this case Symonds becomes prophetic in relation to the future removal of the appendix in similar cases. I have found but three other instances of operation upon the appendix stopping short of its removal. Morton,[242] on April 27, 1887, removed the larger part of an appendix containing a perforation, between two ligatures, one applied near the base and one near the distal free end of the appendix.   Sands,[309] on December 31, 1887, closed a perforation of the appendix by suture.   Tait,[341] in 1889, slit open and drained an appendix.   All three patients recovered.

Excision of the Appendix.—Kroenlein,[184] on February 14, 1884, performed the first removal of the appendix for acute appendicitis.   He was followed in 1886 by Weir,[361] Bryant,[51] and one or two others. These earliest appendicectomies for acute appendicitis had one discouraging feature in common; they were all fatal.

The first successful removal of the appendix was performed by Hall,[143] on May 8, 1886, in an operation for the relief of a strangulated hernia.   The appendix, with an abscess around it, was found among the contents of the hernial sac, tied off, and removed.

Morton,[212] on March 19, 1888, and Sands,[309] on April 17, 1888, performed the first successful appendicectomies for acute appendicitis, the correct diagnosis having been made in both cases before operation. To Morton belongs priority of performance, to Sands priority of publication.   Other successful appendicectomies for acute appendicitis were performed during 1888, in the order named, by Hoffmann,[158] McBurney,[212] Cutler,[71] and Weir.[361]   Hoffmann removed the appendix through a median incision, and the case of McBurney was the first in which an acutely inflamed appendix, full of pus, was removed entire and without rupture.

Thereafter removal of the appendix in acute appendicitis rapidly became a recognized and oft-undertaken procedure.   As early as 1889, McBurney[219] reported seven appendicectomies of his own with six recoveries and one death, and Morton[213] four appendicectomies with two recoveries and two deaths.   Since that time scores of operators number their appendicectomies for acute appendicitis by the hundreds.

Treves,[346] on June 29, 1888, performed the first appendicectomy for relapsing appendicitis. The operation as described would be classed as modern even at this day, the stump end being closed by suture instead of ligated, the abdominal wall closed for primary union, and the patient recovering. The rapidity with which operations for relapsing appendicitis, or interval operations, were adopted, and the success with which they were practised by surgeons the world over, are best evidenced by the fact that Bull,[47] as early as 1894, was able to collect four hundred and forty-four interval operations with eight deaths. It is safe to say that at the present day several thousand such cases could be collected from the literature alone.

The Technics of Appendicectomy.—The various surgical procedures for the simple evacuation and drainage of a peri-appendicular abscess have already been considered. It remains to record the history of the development of the technics of the operation for the removal of the appendix.

Appendicectomy for Acute Perforative or Gangrenous Appendicitis.—During the two or three years immediately following the first removal of the appendix for acute perforative appendicitis by Kroenlein,[184] in 1884, and the early, equally unsuccessful imitations of his example, the advocates of appendicectomy in pus cases were few indeed. The first successful cases, reported in 1888, furnished a new stimulus to surgical activity in this direction, and within two or three years thereafter the number of cases reported slowly increased. Since 1890 the large majority of surgeons with a name advocate removal of the appendix in acute appendicitis as the routine procedure, always to be attempted save under most exceptional conditions. A few surgeons claim that it is always both possible and better to remove the appendix in acute appendicitis. This advice and practice are based upon the fact that a second operation for appendicitis has become necessary in some cases in which the appendix was left at the first operation. Comparatively, however, the cases in which such a secondary operation was called for or performed are very few. Morton,[243] Patel,[203] Homans,[160] and Wolf[369] among others have put on record such secondary operations. The expedient adopted by Wyeth[374] of operating at two sittings represents an unnecessary compromise.

In direct opposition to the modern tendency to remove the appendix whenever feasible, and vainly attempting to stem the tide, we find Barton,[21] as late as 1894, and a few others even more recently, preaching the doctrine of leaving the appendix in operations for acute appendicitis, claiming better results from this practice. That this claim does not hold good in the work of the better operators goes without saying.

The Incision in Acute Appendicitis.—The early incisions employed in operations for acute appendicitis, when abscesses were emptied and drained only, as well as when the appendix was removed, always divided all the various anatomical layers of the abdominal wall in one and the same directions: either a little above and parallel to Poupart's ligament, or nearly vertically, just external and parallel to the outer border of the right rectus abdominis muscle. Aside from the counter-opening in the back more or less frequently practised by a number of surgeons, Dejacé[83] in one case practised lumbar incision of a perityphlitic abscess, and Gerster[130] speaks of Lange as in one instance having to abstain from removing the appendix through an anterior incision, later on removing the organ successfully through a posterior wound. Vischer,[360] in 1897, proposed a new site for the incision, placing it above and parallel to the iliac crest and running from the outer edge of the external oblique inward to the anterior superior iliac spine. The median incision has also been practised, now and then, by Hoffmann[158] and others, but has found no enthusiastic advocates.

The gridiron incision of McBurney,[223] published in 1894, represents the most modern thought and fully satisfactory technics in regards to the incision of the anterior abdominal wall practised anywhere between the outer borders of the recti and the erector spinæ muscles on either side, not only for appendicitis, either acute or chronic, but also for other intra-abdominal conditions exceptionally best approached within the limits stated. McBurney at first thought his incision unsuitable for pus cases calling for gauze packing. This judgment, however, has been reversed by the further experience of a number of American operators, among them the writer, who constantly use this incision in cases of acute appendicitis, and consider all the other incisions already mentioned as antiquated and out of place in up-to-date surgery. The slight modification of the gridiron incision proposed by Elliot,[108] who cuts the fascia of the external oblique horizontally, while attempting to refine on the principle enunciated by McBurney, is of no practical importance.

The Incision in Chronic Appendicitis.—The comments made anent the first incisions practised for acute appendicitis hold good also for those made for the removal of the appendix in interval cases, with this important exception: that, beginning with the very first removal of the appendix for recurrent inflammation by Treves, the abdominal wound has been very generally closed for primary union without attempts at drainage. The gridiron incision, originally devised and brought forward by McBurney for cases of appendicitis not requiring drainage, but equally applicable to pus cases, represents the first giant stride forward in the surgery of the incision made for the removal of the appendix in chronic appendicitis. Battle,[23] in 1895, gave us the incision through the right rectus abdominis muscle, which in chronic appendicitis has become the successful rival of the gridiron incision of McBurney. The rectus incision of Battle may be found admirably pictured and described as the simple incision by Deaver[70] in 1896. Curiously enough, in 1897, Jalaguier,[166] Kammerer,[127] and Lennander[105] published the Battle incision, each apparently under the impression that the incision was original with himself. The lumbar incision for chronic appendicitis was brought forward by Edebohls,[100] in 1898, as applicable to cases in which right nephropexy and appendicectomy were called for in the same patient.

About ten centimetres seems to be the length of incision usually accepted as required in acute appendicitis. In the surgery of chronic appendicitis Morris,[239] in 1893, first recognized that such long incisions were unnecessary, and loudly called for the one-and-a-half-inch incision. He has since been outdone in this direction by Scott,[314] who writes on "the incision less than one and a half inches long in appendicitis." The writer[103] has recently recorded his views on the subject, and will close with the statement that the only incisions necessary and permissible in the modern surgery of the appendix are the gridiron incision of McBurney, the rectus incision of Battle, and, perhaps, the lumbar incision of Edebohls.

Technics of the Stump.—The treatment of the stump left after amputation of the appendix has occupied a great deal of the attention of surgeons. In some cases of acute appendicitis, with gangrenous destruction and disintegration of the entire appendix and even of greater or less areas of the cæcal walls, the question of a stump and its treatment does not arise. In such cases the damage must be repaired by suture, and the danger must be minimized by the usual gauze packing and drainage, or by suture of the damaged bowel to the abdominal wall as practised by Byrd,[52] Bunner,[40] and others. Simple ligation of the stump, though still very generally practised, cannot be considered a perfectly safe procedure. Dock[80] has put on record a death from simple ligation, and the writer knows of another unpublished case in which intestinal leakage and fatal peritonitis followed the slipping of a ligature placed around an appendix stump.

The example of Lautard,[199] who amputated the tip of the appendix and sewed the long stump to the abdominal walls, has found no imitators.

Invagination of the ligated stump has been attempted by Smith[58] and many others since his time. All such attempts are illogical and have necessarily met with failure, as complete invagination of a ligated stump is an impossibility. The most that can be accomplished is to depress a ligated stump and cover it over with peritoneum, a procedure which Stimson[337] was the first to condemn as "bottling up" of the appendix.

Closure of the open ends of the appendix by suture was practised by Treves[340] in the very first case of removal of the appendix for recurrent appendicitis, the mucous and muscular coats being united by suture. Treves, however, found it impossible in his case to sew the peritoneum over the free end of the stump, which procedure appears to have been first accomplished by Allingham. Monks,[236] in 1890, improved this step of the technique by first inverting the cut end of the appendix and then closing the inverted edge by suture. Ruth,[300] in 1895, sutured the cut edges of the appendix stump, inverted the stump, and approximated the peritoneum by suture.

Inversion of the appendix stump without previous ligation and suture was practised by Dawbarn[76] as far back as 1890 or 1891. The correct principle underlying Dawbarn's method was clumsily imitated by Plummer,[276] who slits the appendix stump upward at two opposite points, trims and inverts the flaps, and sutures the serosa—and by Bloch,[38] who uses a temporary suture through the lips of the appendix stump, passes the threaded suture through the cæcal wall opposite the appendix, from within outward, withdraws the suture, and closes the peritoneum over the inverted stump.

Price[284] and Eastman[94] do away entirely with a stump by excision of the entire appendix and suture of the resultant hole in the bowel wall. Edebohls[99] originated inversion of the entire, uncut appendix, the only procedure which does away with the necessity of opening the bowel and with the resultant risk of infection. His procedure, so far as I am aware, has found but one imitator, Fowler,[121] whose first and only case of inversion of the entire appendix for chronic appendicitis ended fatally as the result of the operation. Against this, however, stand considerably more than one hundred cases of inversion of the entire, uncut appendix for chronic appendicitis, at my own hands, without a single death.

Septic Peritonitis; Drainage; Accidents.—The treatment of the diffuse septic peritonitis accompanying appendicitis has received attention at several hands. McBurney,[221] in 1895, wrote the most important clinical contribution to this aspect of appendicitis, advocating free flushing of the peritoneum with drainage, procedures practised by Byrd[52] as early as 1881. Pond[278] added to these resources, in extremely bad cases, incision of the intestine and suture of the incision lips to the abdominal wound, permitting of the direct introduction of salines, stimulants, etc., into the intestine.

Gauze drainage is all but universally used in pus cases, either alone or combined with rubber or glass drainage tubes. Morris[240] first employed an iodoform wick, and later a special device consisting of a slender piece of gauze wrapped about with perforated rubber tissue. As regards the use of iodoform gauze, opinions of experienced men vary widely. Morris, for instance, in 1897, published a tirade against the use of gauze, iodoform and plain, while Murphy, in the same year, returns to the use of iodoform gauze after having completely discarded it for a time.

Very recently a tendency to close immediately the

abdominal wall for primary union in some cases of appendicitis with pus is becoming manifest. Schueller,[313] in 1889, was the first, I believe, successfully to close the abdomen at once and entirely after an appendicectomy at which he found turbid serum in the peritoneal cavity. Clark,[55] in 1897, alludes to instances of similar practice, and Boldt informs me that he has several times operated successfully in the same manner in cases in which a small amount of pus was present.

A curious accident, tearing off of the distal end of the appendix during enucleation of the latter, and failure to find again the distal end, is recorded by Huntington.[163] The writer has had a similar experience; both cases ended in recovery, without drainage. Hutchinson[162] reports an operative case in which he found the appendix at some distance from the cæcum, from which it had entirely separated by sloughing.

Statistical.—Autopsy statistics of appendicitis, large and important for the time at which they were presented, have been given by Leudet,[201] Finnell,[115] Toft,[314] Fitz,[116] Einhorn,[105] Wallis,[356] Ribbert,[287] and Robinson.[295] Kleinwaechter[197] and With[367] have furnished statistics regarding the duration of appendicitis under medical treatment, while Sands[308] and Fitz[117] investigated the mortality under medical and under surgical treatment. McBurney[221] presents personal statistics of operations for appendicitis in the presence of diffuse septic peritonitis. Von Mayer[354] gives us a very unique, practical, and interesting study of seventy-five operative cases of chronic appendicitis. Of these, thirty-three presented clinical symptoms corresponding to the lesions found, thirty-two presented no clinical symptoms, and ten had severe symptoms with no lesions. Statistics of operative cases, with mortality, have been published by Clay,[59] Bull,[47] MacDonald,[213] Murphy,[252] Johnson,[169] Kuemmell,[188] Sonnenburg,[330] Deaver,[60] Halliday,[144] and very numerous others.

Illustrations.—Appendicitis has furnished a favor-
ite subject for the artist's pencil and brush, and it is
not too much to say that perhaps upon no other subject in the entire range of pathology has such wide-
spread, profuse, elaborate, and beautiful illustration
been lavished. I call attention in the following to
those illustrations which have struck me as particu-
larly noteworthy; they constitute, however, only a
modicum of the whole.

The anatomy of the appendix and its vicinity has
been thoroughly illustrated by Little,[208] Schueller,[313]
Lockwood and Rolleston,[209] Levings,[202] Kelynack,[177]
and Jonnesco.[168] The general pathology has been
well pictured by Fenger,[112] Fowler,[121] Jessop,[167] Plummer,[276] Lannelongue,[192] Smith,[326] and Sonnenburg[328]
among others, while the histo-pathology has been especially well delineated by Letulle and Weinberg.[200]
Chronic appendicitis has received the artistic atten-
tions of Foges[118]; interval appendicitis those of Abbe';
appendicitis obliterans those of Senn[318] and Zuckerkandl[370]; and the location of abscesses those of Harris.[117] Intestinal strangulation following appendicitis
has been pictured by most of those already enumerated
as having described cases, while some of the operative
sequelæ have been delineated by Peck.[261] Cysts and
cystic degeneration of the appendix have been well
pictured by Gruber,[130] Gouillioud,[130] Shoemaker,[321]
Sonnenburg,[327] and Coats.[63]

Among illustrations of other pathological conditions
affecting the appendix the following may be mentioned: Invagination of the appendix, by McKidd[228];
prolapse of mucous membrane of the appendix, by
Rolleston[300]; thrombosis of appendicular vessels, by
Dieulafoy[87]; tuberculosis of the appendix, by Apert[10];
and primary cancer of the appendix, by Mosse and
Daunic.[247] The technics of the operation for appendicitis have been abundantly illustrated by many
writers, among others by Ruth,[300] Deaver,[73] Fowler,[121]

and Morris.[240]   The article of Ruth contains beautiful illustrations detailing the technics of the stump. Deaver's admirable plates are the only ones I have found illustrating the rectus incision.   Five cuts detailing post-operative sequelæ in a very interesting case are given by Peck.[264]

Literature.—The entire literature of appendicitis, complete to the beginning of the year 1899, and including, in addition, about fifty numbers appearing during the present year, has been consulted in the preparation of this article.   This vast literature embraces, as already stated, more than twenty-five hundred journal articles, dissertations, and books.   A complete bibliography, prepared by the author, may be found in the library of the New York Academy of Medicine, where it is at the disposal of any one who may wish to consult it.

The appended bibliography of three hundred and seventy-six references is believed to include nearly all of real value that has been published upon the subject of appendicitis.   It includes papers and books important and valuable for the time at which they were published, together with a number of articles to which reference became necessary in the preparation of this historical review.

BIBLIOGRAPHY.

1. Abbe, R.: MEDICAL RECORD, New York, 1897, lii., 37–39.
2. Abrahams, R.: Amer. Jour. of Obst., 1897, xxxv., 205–225.
3. Achard, C.: Mercredi méd., Paris, 1894, v., 569–572.
4. Achard, C., et Broca, A.: Bull. et mém. soc. méd. des hôp. de Paris, 1897, s. 3, xiv., 442.
5. Adenot: Compt. rend. soc. de biol., Paris, 1891, s. 9, iii., 740–742.
6. Ahrt: Jour. d. Chir. u. Augenh., Berlin, 1835, xxiii., 140–148.
7. Albers, T. F. H.: Beobacht. a. d. Gebiete d. Pathol., 8vo, Bonn, 1838, pt. 2, 1–37.

8. Allen, D. P.: Rev. de gynécol. et de chir. abd., Paris, 1897, i., 665–690.

9. Andrews, T. II.: Proceedings of the Path. Soc. of Philadelphia, 1866, ii., 238–240.

10. Apert, E.: Presse méd., Paris. 1898, ii., 343.

11. Ardouard : Progrès méd., Paris, 1876, iv., 416.

12. Ashby, H.: Lancet, London, 1879, ii., 649.

13. Atkinson, G. A.: British Med. Jour., London, 1895, i., 1439.

14. Aufrecht, E.: Berlin. klin. Wochenschr., 1869, vi., 308.

15. Baernhof, A.: Beitr. z. Heilk., Riga, 1854–55, iii., 147–150.

16. Baillet : Bull. soc. anat. de Paris, 1891, lxvi., 67.

17. Baldy, J. M.: Medical News, Philadelphia, 1889, lv., 579–581.

18. Bamberger : Verhandl. d. phys.-med. Gesellsch. in Würzb., 1859, ix., 123.

19. Bartholow, R.: Amer. Jour. of Med. Sci., Philadelphia, 1866, n. s., lii., 351–362.

20. Barlow and Godlee : Trans. Clin. Soc. of London, 1885–86, xix., 88–94.

21. Barton, J. M.: Philadelphia Polyclinic, 1894, iii., 173–175.

22. Battersby, F.: Dublin Quarterly Jour. of Med. Sci., 1847, iii., 516–539.

23. Battle, W. H.: British Med. Jour., London, 1895, ii., 1360.

24. Battle, W. H.: British Med. Jour., London, 1897, i. 965–967.

25. Bayley, N. B.: MEDICAL RECORD, New York, 1895, xlvii., 342.

26. Beaussenat, M.: Rev. de gynéc. et de chir. abd., Paris, 1897, i. 283–312.

27. Beck, C.: New York Med. Jour., 1898, lxviii., 685, 727, 757, 810.

28. Bennett, R.: Trans. Path. Soc., London, 1852–53, iv., 146.

29. Berard : Gaz. des hôp., Paris, 1840, 2me s., ii., 145.

30. Beurnier, L.: Jour. de méd. de Paris, 1898, 2me s., x., 546.

31. Biegi : Méd. moderne, Paris, 1897, viii., 643.

32. Bierbaum, J.: Jour. f. Kinderk., Erlangen, 1867, xlviii., 26–55.

33. Bierhoff, C.: Ueber die Krankheiten des Wurmfortsatzes, 8vo, Ludenscheid, 1878.

34. Bierhoff, C.: Deutsches Arch. f. klin. Med., Leipzig, 1880–81, xxvii., 248–267.

35. Biggs, H. M.: MEDICAL RECORD, New York, 1888, xxxiii., 720.

36. Binkley, J. T.: Amer. Jour. of Obst., New York, 1894, xxix., 474, 493.
37. Birch-Hirschfeld, F. v.: Arch. d. Heilk., Leipzig, 1871, xii,, 191.
38. Bloch, A. J. N.: New Orleans Med. and Surg. Jour., 1896–97, xlix , 75–78.
39. Bloomfield, J. E.: British Med. Jour., London, 1895, ii., 658.
40. Boardman. C. H.: Northwest. Med. and Surg. Jour., St. Paul, 1873–74, iv., 8–12.
41. Bontecou R. B.: Trans. Med. Soc. of New York, Albany, 1873, lxvii., 137–139.
42. Boussi, R : France méd., Paris, 1878. xxv., 154–156.
43. Buck, G.: Amer. Med. Times, New York, 1861, iii., 258–260.
44. Buck, G.: Trans. New York Acad. of Med. (1874–76), 1876, 2d s , ii., 1–14.
45. Bull, W. T.: New York Med. Jour., 1873, xviii., 240–264.
46. Bull, W. T.: Medical Record, New York, 1886, xxix., 265.
47. Bull, W. T.: Medical Record, New York, 1894, xlv., 385–389.
48. Burne, E.: Gaz. méd. de Paris, 1838, 2me s., vi., 385–401.
49. Brenner, A.: Wien. klin. Wochenschr., 1888, i , 216–219.
50. Bryant, J. D.: Annals of Surgery, Philadelphia, 1893, xvii., 164–180.
51. Bryant, J. D.: Gaillard's Med. Jour., New York, 1887, xliv , 134–136.
52. Byrd. W. A.: Trans. Amer. Med. Assoc., Philadelphia, 1881, xxxii., 433–437.
53. Cameron, H. C.: Glasgow Med. Jour., 1894, xlii., 143–147.
54. Carless, A.: Kings College Hosp. Rep., 1894–95, London, 1896, ii., 93.
55. Clark, J. G.: Amer. Jour. of Obst., 1897, xxxv., 672.
56. Clark, A.: Amer. Med. Times, New York. 1861, ii , 258.
57. Clarke, E. W.: Med. Press and Cir., London, 1894, n. s., lvii , 386–388.
58. Clarke and Smith: Lancet, London, 1890, i., 956–958.
59. Clay, D. M.: New Orleans Med. and Surg. Jour., 1878–79, vi., 196–214.
60. Clemens, T.: Deutsche Klinik, Berlin, 1851. iii., 85.
61. Cless : Med. Cor.-Bl. d. württb. ärztl. Ver., Stuttgart, 1847 xvii , 27.
62. Cless, Jr.: Med. Cor.-Bl. d. württb. ärztl. Ver., Stuttgart, 1857, xxvii., 25, 33.
63. Coats, J.: Manual of Pathology, third edition, 1895,

Longmans, Green & Co., London, 8vo, p. 1130 (pp. 863 and 876).

64. Coe, H. C.: New York Polyclinic, 1894. iv., 73.

65. Combemarle : Bull. méd. du Nord, Lille, 1891, xxx., 223–225.

66. Courtney, W.: Northwestern Lancet, St. Paul, 1897, xvii., 443–446.

67. Craig, C. F.: New England Medical Monthly, 1897, xvi., 407–417.

68. Crutcher, H.: Medical Era, Chicago, 1896, xiii., 312.

69. Crutcher, H.: International Journal of Surgery, New York, 1896, ix , 99.

70. Crutcher, H.: Hahnemannian Advocate, Chicago, 1896, xxxv., 277–283.

71. Cutler, E. R.: Boston Med. and Surg. Jour., 1889, cxx., 554–556.

72 Czerny and Heddaeus : Beitrag z. klin. Chir., Tübingen, 1898, xxi., 513–618.

73. Dade, W. H.: Medical News, New York, 1898, lxxii., 439.

74. Dale : British Med. Jour , London, 1879. ii , 655.

75. Davat . Bull. soc. anat. de Paris, 1873, xlviii., 577.

76. Dawbarn, R. H. M.: MEDICAL RECORD, New York, 1895, xlviii., 289–294.

77. Deaver, J. B.: Medical News, Philadelphia, 1894, lxiv., 533, 566.

78. Deaver, J. B.: Trans. Med. Soc. of Pennsylvania, Philadelphia, 1894, xxv., 110–118.

79. Deaver, J. B.: A Treatise on Appendicitis, Philadelphia, 1896, P. Blakiston, Son & Co., 168 pages, 32 plates. 8vo.

80 Deaver, J. B.: New Orleans Med. and Sur. Jour., 1898–99. li., 443–445.

81. Deaver, J. B.: Trans. Amer. Assoc. of Obstet. and Gynæcologists, 1897, Philadelphia, 1897, x., 362–372.

82. De Gennes, P.: Bull. soc. anat. de Paris, 1883, lviii., 168–172.

83. Dejacé, L.: Ann. soc. méd.-chir. de Liège, 1894, xxxiii., 282–285.

84. Delbet, P.: Leçons de clinique chirurgicale, Paris, 1899, G. Steinheil, 8vo, 376 pages.

85. Dennis, F. S.: Trans. Amer. Surg. Assoc., Philadelphia, 1890, viii., 135–166.

86. Diagnosis (The) and Treatment of Inflammation of the Appendix ; a discussion. Med. Communications of the Massachusetts Med. Soc., Boston, 1891, xv., 529–560.

87. Dieulafoy : Clin. méd. de l'Hôtel-Dieu de Paris (1897–98), 1899, 2, 167.

88. Dieulafoy, G.: Presse méd., Paris, 1898, ii., 281–284.
89. Dock, G.: Medical Age, Detroit, 1892, x., 397–402.
90. Draper, F. W.: Boston Med. and Surg. Jour., 1884, cx., 131.
91. Duncan, J.: Trans. Med.-Chir. Soc., Edinburgh, 1892–93, n. s., xii., 227–237.
92. Dupré, E.: France méd., Paris, 1888, i., 25–31.
93. Dupuytren: Clinique chirurgicale, Paris, 1839, iii., 8vo, 520.
94. Eastman, J.: Western Med. Rec., 1899, iv., 43–48.
95. Edebohls, G. M.: Mediz. Monatschr., 1890, ii., 220.
96. Edebohls, G. M.: Amer. Jour. of Med. Sci., 1894, n. s., cvii., 487.
97. Edebohls, G. M.: Post-Graduate, 1894, ix., 154.
98. Edebohls, G. M.: Amer. Jour. of Obst., 1895, xxxi., 164.
99. Edebohls, G. M.: Amer. Jour. of Med. Sci., 1895, n. s., cix., 650.
100. Edebohls, G. M.: Centralbl. f. Gyn., 1898, xxii., 1084–1090.
101. Edebohls, G. M.: Post Graduate, 1899, xiv., 85–98.
102. Edebohls, G. M.: MEDICAL RECORD, New York, 1899, lv., 341–345.
103. Edebohls, G. M.: MEDICAL RECORD, New York, 1899, lv., 665–667.
104. Edson, B.: Proceedings of Med. Soc. of County of Kings, Brooklyn, 1879–80, iv., 45–49.
105. Einhorn, H.: Münchner med. Wochenschr., 1891, xxxviii, 121, 140.
106. Ekehorn, G.: Upsala Laekaref. Foerh., 1892–93, xxviii., 113–150.
107. Eliot, G.: Proceedings of Conn. Med. Soc., Bridgeport, 1893, 194–199.
108. Elliot, J. W.: Boston Med. and Surg. Jour., 1896, cxxxv., 433, 441–445.
109. Ellis, R.: New York Med. Jour., 1899, lxxv., 90–92.
110. Englisch: Bericht d. k. k. Krankenanst. Rudolfstift. in Wien, 1878, 391
111. Faisans: Bull. et mém. soc. méd. des hôp. de Paris, 1895, 3me s, xiii., 228–239.
112. Fenger, C.: Amer. Jour of Obst., New York, 1893, xxviii, 161–199.
113. Fenwick, S.: Lancet, London, 1884, ii., 987, 1039.
114. Féré: Progrès méd., Paris, 1877, v., 73.
115. Finnell, T. C.: MEDICAL RECORD, New York, 1869, iv., 65.
116. Fitz, R. H.: Amer. Jour. of Med. Sci., Philadelphia, 1886, n. s., xcii., 321–346.

117. Fitz, R. H.: Boston Med. and Surg. Jour., 1890, cxxii., 619.

118. Foges, A.: Wien. med. Wochensch., 1896, xlvi., 2169, 2227, 2281, 2329.

119. Fowler, G. R.: Medical News, Philadelphia, 1893, lxiii., 604.

120. Fowler, G. R.: Annals of Surgery, Philadelphia, 1894, xix., 4, 146, 327, 474, 546, 3 plates.

121. Fowler, G. R.: Amer. Jour. of Med. Sci., Philadelphia, 1897, n. s., cxiii., 152–157.

122. Fowler, G. R.: Brooklyn Med. Jour., 1897, xi., 243–259.

123. Fowler, G. R.: Jour. Amer. Med. Assoc., Chicago, 1897, xxix , 933–940.

124. Fowler, G. R.: Meth. Episcop. Hosp. Rep., 1887–97, New York, 1898, i., 164–211, 7 plates.

125. Fox, R. H : Lancet, London, 1885, ii., 1166.

126. Frazer, J. E.: British Med. Jour., London, 1895, i., 1320.

127. Freeman, C.: Canada Lancet, Toronto, 1871–72, iv., 268.

128. Freiberg, A. H.: Ohio Med. Jour., Cincinnati, 1896, vii., 220 227

129. Gangolph et Duplant : Rev. de chir., Paris, 1897, xvii., 503–518.

130. Gerster, A. G.: New York Med. Jour., 1890, lii., 6–14.

131. Gerster, A. G.: Philadelphia Monthly Med. Jour., 1899, i., 170–174.

132. Gibney, V. P.: Amer. Jour. of Med. Sci., Philadelphia, 1881, n. s , lxxxi., 119–128.

133. Glantenay : Presse méd., Paris, 1899, i., 9.

134. Glazebrook, L. W.: Virginia Med. Monthly, Richmond, 1895–96, xxii., 211.

135. Goluboff : Berlin. klin. Wochenschr., 1897, xxxiv., 9–11.

136. Gouillioud : Lyon médicale, 1891, lxvii., 245–254, 1 plate.

137. Grandin, E. H. : Amer. Gynæc. Jour., Toledo, 1893, iii., 544–548.

138. Gross, H. : Deutsche Zeitschr. f. Chir., Leipzig, 1898, xlvii., 260–265.

139. Gruber, W. : Arch. f. pathol. Anat., etc., Berlin, 1875, lxiii., 97–99.

140. Guinard, A. : Gaz. des hôp., Paris, 1896, lxix., 1350–1352.

141. Guttmann, P. : Deutsche med. Wochensch., Leipzig, 1891, xvii., 260.

142. Habershon: Observation on Diseases of the Alimentary Canal, London, 1857.

143. Hall, R. J.: New York Med. Jour., 1886, xliii., 662.
144. Halliday, J. C.: British Med. Jour., London, 1898, i., 1195.
145. Halsted, W. S.: Johns Hopkins Hosp. Bull., Baltimore, 1894, v., 113.
146. Hancock H.: London Med. Gazette, 1848, n. s., vii., 547–550.
147. Harris, M. L.: Jour. Amer. Med. Assoc., Chicago, 1895, xxv., 1085–1088.
148. Harte, R. H.: American Lancet, Detroit, 1894, n. s., xviii., 294.
149. Hartley, F.: MEDICAL RECORD, New York, 1890, xxxviii., 169–174.
150. Hartmann et Reymond : Assoc. franç. d'urol., Proc.-verb., 1897, Paris, 1898, ii., 324–330.
151. Hawkins, H. P.: On Diseases of the Vermiform Appendix, etc., London, 1895, Macmillan & Co., 146 pages. 8vo.
152. Hektoen, L.: Amer. Jour. of Obst., New York, 1893, xxviii., 272–280.
153. Hendricks, H. W.: MEDICAL RECORD, New York, 1876, xi., 764.
154. Hewson, A.: Amer. Jour. of Med. Sci., Philadelphia, 1893, n. s , cvi., 185–190.
155. Hind, W.: Prov. Med. Jour., Leicester, 1895, xiv., 489.
156. Hirst, B. C.: Amer. Jour. Gyn. and Pæd., 1890–91, iv., 39.
157. Hodenpyl, E.: New York Med. Jour., 1893, lviii , 777–785.
158. Hoffmann, J.: Amer. Jour. of Obst., New York, 1888, xxi., 1185–1188.
159. Homans, J.: Boston Med. and Surg. Jour., 1886, cxiv., 388.
160. Homans, J. : Boston Med. and Surg. Jour., 1890, cxxii., 54, 77.
161. Homans, J.: Boston Med. and Surg. Jour., 1899, cxl., 112.
162. Hutchinson, J. A. : Montreal Med. Jour., 1899, xxviii., 205.
163. Huntington, T. W.: Occidental Med. Times, Sacramento, 1894, viii., 12–17.
164. Jackson : Extr. Rec. Bost. Soc. Med. Improvement, 1859, iv., 49–52.
165. Jaggard, W.: Amer. Jour. of Obst., New York, 1893, xxviii., 265–269.
166. Jalaguier, A.: Presse médicale, Paris, 1897, v., 53.
167. Jessop, T. R.: British Med. Jour., London, 1894, i., 627–637, 1 plate.

168. Jonnesco and Juvara: Progrès médical, Paris, 1894, xix., 273, 303, 321, 353, 369, 4 plates.

169. Johnson, M. M.: Jour. Amer. Med. Assoc., Chicago, 1896, xxvi, 1202–1206.

170. Jorand, A.: Bull. soc. anat. de Paris, 1894, lxix., 300–303.

171. Josué : Compt. rend. soc. de biol., Paris, 1897, 10me s., iv., 280–282.

172. Kammerer, F.: Annals of Surgery, Philadelphia, 1897, xxvi., 225–228.

173. Karewski, F. : Deutsche med. Wochenschr., Leipzig and Berlin, 1897, xxiii., 294, 312, 331 ; Ver.-Beil. 67 (Discussion), Ver.-Beil. 69-72.

174. Kayser, F. : Hygiea, Stockholm, 1896, lviii., pt. 2, 557–560.

175. Keen, W. W.: Philadelphia Med. Jour., 1898, i., 764.

176. Keen, W. W.: Trans. Amer. Surg. Assoc., Philadelphia, 1898, xvi., 243–252.

177. Kelynack, T. N. : The Pathology of the Vermiform Appendix, London, 1893, H. K. Lewis, 223 pages, 8vo.

178. Kelly, H. A.: Operative Gynæcology, New York, D. Appleton & Co., vol. i., p. 123.

179. Kleinwaechter : Mitt. a. d. Grenzgeb. d. Med. u. Chir., Jena, 1896, i., 717–728.

180. Kolb : Med. Cor.-Bl. d. württemb. ärztl. Ver., Stuttgart, 1860, xxx., 103.

181. Kottmann, A.: Cor.-Bl. f. schweizer Aerzte, 1871, i., 8.

182. Krafft, C. : Rev. méd. de la Suisse rom., Genève, 1893, xiii., 764–772.

183. Krakowitzer, E.: New York Medical Jour., 1871, xiii., 733–736.

184. Kroenlein, R. U.: Arch. f. klin. Chir., 1886, xxxiii., 514.

185. Kroenlein, R. U.: Arch. f. klin. Chir., Berlin, 1877, xxi. (Suppl.-Heft), 165.

186. Kuester : Centralbl. f. Chir., Leipzig, 1898, xxv., 1241–1243.

187. Kuemmell, H.: Arch. f. klin. Chir., 1890, xl., 618.

188. Kuemmell, H.: Berlin. klin. Wochenschr., 1898, xxxv., 321–328.

189. Kuemmell, H. : Deutsche med. Wochenschr., Leipzig u. Berlin, 1898, xxiv., V. B. 181.

190. Lang : Med. Corresp.-Bl. d. württemb. ärztl. Ver., Stuttgart, 1860, xxx., 103.

191. Landsberg : Allg. med. Centr.-Ztg., Berlin, 1846, xv., 809–814.

192. Lannelongue : Gaz. hebdom. de méd., Paris, 1883, 2me s., xx., 33–46, 1 plate.

193. Lautard : Arch. prov. de chir., Paris, 1895, iv., 712–717.
194. Legg, J. W.: St. Bartholomew's Hospital Report, London, 1880, xvi., 259.
195. Leguen, F.: De l'appendicite, Paris, 1897, Masson et Cie., 40 pages, 8vo.
196. Leidy, J.: Medical News, Philadelphia. 1894, lxv., 357.
197. Lemariey : Gaz. des hôp., Paris. 1893, lxvi., 1318–1320.
198. Lennander, K. : Upsala Laekaref. Foerh., 1898, xxvii., 87–103.
199. Lennander, K. G. : Centralb. f. Chir., 1898, xxv., 90.
200. Letulle, M., et M. Weinberg : Arch. des sc. méd. de Bucarest, Paris, 1897, ii., 360–510.
201. Leudet, T. E.: Arch. gén. de méd., Paris, 1859, ii., 139, 315.
202. Levings, A. H.: Trans. Wisc. Med. Soc., Madison, 1892, xxvi, 60–82.
203. Lewis, G.: New York Jour. of Med., 1856, 3 s., i., 328–353.
204. Lewis, J. C.: MEDICAL RECORD, New York, 1894, xlvi., 463.
205. Lieberkühn, J. N.: De Valvulâ coli usu Processus Vermicularis, Ludg. Bat., 1739.
206. Lincoln, II. M. : Amer. Jour. of Med. Sci., Philadelphia, 1853, n. s., xxvi., 364.
207. Little, T. E. : Dublin Quar. Jour. Med. Sci., 1871, lii., 237–241.
208. Little : Lancet, London, 1847, i., 389.
209. Lockwood, C. B. and Rolleston, H. D.: Jour. of Anat. and Physiology, London. 1891-92, xxvi., 130-148, 1 plate.
210. Long, W. J.: Intercolonial Med. Jour. Australasia, Melbourne, 1896, i., 708.
211. Long, J. W.: Medical Review, St. Louis, 1894, xxx., 441-445.
212. Lop : Rev. de méd., Paris, 1897, xvii., 648–652.
213. MacDonald, W. G.: Trans. Assoc. Amer. Obst. and Gynec., Philadelphia, 1895, vii., 131-144.
214. Machell, H. T.: Canadian Practitioner, Toronto, 1890, xv., 537–543.
215. Mader, J.: Ber. d. k. k. Krankenanst. Rudolfstift. in Wien (1876), 1877, 382.
216. Matthieu, A.: Gaz. des hôp., Paris, 1896, lxix., 402-404.
217. Maylard : Trans. Glasgow Pathol. and Clin. Soc., 1891-93. iv., 111.
218. McArthur, L.L.: Amer. Jour. of Obst., New York, 1895, xxxi , 181-185.
219. McBurney, C.: New York Med. Jour., 1889, l., 676-684.

220. McBurney, C.: MEDICAL RECORD, New York, 1892, xli., 421–427.

221. McBurney, C.: MEDICAL RECORD, New York, 1895, xlvii., 385–390.

222. McBurney, C.: New York Med. Jour., 1888, xlvii., 719–721.

223 McBurney, C.: Annals of Surgery, Philadelphia, 1894, xx., 38-43.

224. McCallum, H. A.: Medical News, Philadelphia, 1892, lxi., 681.

225 McCosh and Hawkes : Amer. Jour. of Med. Sci., 1897, cxiii., 513.

226. McGraw, T. A.: British Med. Jour., London, 1897, ii., 956–958.

227 McGuire, H.: Virginia Med. Monthly, Richmond, 1895–96, xxii., 885–903.

228. McKidd, J.: Edinburgh Med. Jour., 1859, iv., 2, 793, 2 plates.

229 McPhedran, A.: Canada Lancet, Toronto, 1896–97, xxix., 115–117.

230. Meek, H.: New York Polyclinic, 1895, v.-vi., 210.

231. Merling, F. · Diss. sistens processus vermiformis anato-miam pathologicam, Heidelbergæ, 4to, 1836.

232. Mestivier, M.: Jour. de méd., chir., phar., etc., Paris, 1759, x 441.

233. Mikulicz, T.: Volkmann's Samml. klin. Vortr., 1885, No. 262, p. 2313.

234. Mixter, S. J.: Boston Med. and Surg. Jour., 1891, cxxv , 697.

235. Moers: Deutsches Arch. f. klin. Med., Leipzig, 1868, iv., 251–256.

236. Monks, G. R.: Boston Med. and Surg. Jour., 1890, cxxii., 543.

237. Monod, C.: Assoc. franç. de chir., Proc.-verb. (etc.), 1894, Paris, 1895, viii., 206–212.

238. Moore, C. H.: Lancet, London, 1864, ii.. 512-515.

239. Morris, R. T.: Trans. Pan-American Medical Congress, 1893, i.. pt. i., 1095-1100.

240. Morris, R. T.: Lectures on Appendicitis, 1899, G. P. Putnam's Sons, 181 pages.

241. Mortier: Jour. compl. du dict. de sc. méd., Paris, 1819, iii., 241–243.

242. Morton, T. G.: Jour. Amer. Med. Assoc., 1888, x., 733-739.

243. Morton, T. G.: Maryland Med. Jour., Baltimore, 1889–90, xxii., 484 ; 1890, xxiii . 8, 89.

244. Morton, T. G.: Trans. College of Physicians, Phila-delphia, 1890, 3 s., xii., 1–36.

245. Morton, T. G.: Jour. Amer. Med. Assoc., Chicago, 1891, xvii., 125–136.

246. Morton, C. A.: Bristol Med.-Chir. Jour., 1897, xv., 319–321, 323

247. Mosse et Daunic: Bull. soc. anat. de Paris, 1897, lxxii., 814.

248. Mott, F. W.: Trans. Pathol. Soc., London, 1888–89, xl., 105.

249 Muenchmeyer: Deutsche Klinik, Berlin, 1860, xii., 43, 56, 81. 93.

250. Mundé, P. F.: MEDICAL RECORD, New York, 1894, xlvi., 678.

251. Murphy, J. B.: Medical News, Philadelphia, 1895, lxvi., 1–8.

252. Murphy, J. B : Jour. Amer. Med. Assoc., Chicago, 1894, xxii., 302, 347, 387, 423.

253. Murray, R. W.: British Med. Jour., London, 1896, ii., 747.

254. Mynter, H.: Appendicitis and its Surgical Treatment, Philadelphia and London, 1897; J. B. Lippincott Company, 303 pages, 8vo.

255. Mynter, H.: Trans of Med. Soc. of New York, 1896, 166–171.

256. Noble, C. P.: Amer. Gynæc. and Obst. Jour., New York, 1895, vii.. 115–117; disc , 146–153.

257 Noyes, R F.: Trans. Rhode Island Med. Soc., 1882, Providence, 1883, ii., pt. 6, 495–539.

258. Nuding, W. H.: Ohio Med. Jour., Cincinnati, 1895, vi., 30–33.

259 Ohlmacher, A. P.: Cleveland Med. Gazette, 1893–94, ix., 511–519.

260. Osler, W.: Montreal Gen. Hosp. Rep., 1880, i., 313.

261. Packard: Proceedings of Pathol. Soc., Philadelphia, 1858, i., 170.

262. Parker, W.: MEDICAL RECORD, New York, 1867, ii., 25–27.

263. Patel, M.: Lyon médicale, 1898, lxxxix., 189–197.

264. Peck, G. S : Trans. Assoc Amer. Obst. and Gynec. (1894), Philadelphia, 1895, vii., 115–130, 5 plates,

265. Peltzer: Deutsche mil.-ärztl. Ztschr., Berlin, 1882, xi., 411.

266. Pepper, W.: Amer. Jour. of Med. Sci., Philadelphia, 1867, n. s., liv., 145–147.

267. Pepper, W.: Trans. Med. Soc. of Pennsylvania, Philadelphia, 1883, xv., 226–246.

268. Perry, J. W.: Memphis Medical Recorder, 1857, v., 659.

269. Peterson, R.: Medical News, Philadelphia. 1893, lxii., 515-517

270. Piersol, G. A.: Univ. Med. Mag., Philadelphia, 1894-95, vii , 893-899.

271. Pierson, W.: Trans. Med. Soc. of New Jersey, Newark, 1871, 279-281.

272. Pilliet and Costes : Bull. soc. anat. de Paris, 1895, lxx., 19-38.

273. Pilliet, A. II. : Progrès médical, Paris, 1898, 3me s., cii., 65-67.

274. Piard, E.: Arch. gén. de méd., Paris, 1896, ii., 290, 436, 560.

275. Pitres, A.: Mém. et bull. soc. méd.-chir. des hôp. de Bordeaux, 1869, iv., 43-49.

276 Plummer, R. H.: Trans. Pan-Amer Med. Congress, 1893, Washington, 1895, pt. ii , 1166-1168, 3 plates.

277. Pollosson, M. : Mém. et compt. rend soc. de sci. méd. de Lyon (1893), 1894, xxxiii., 135-142.

278. Pond. E. M.: Amer. Jour. of Obst. New York, 1898, xxxviii , 829-832.

279 Pond, E. M. : MEDICAL RECORD, New York, 1898, liii., 582-587.

280. Porcher, F. P.: North Carolina Med. Jour., Wilmington. 1879, iv., 375.

281. Porter, W. H.: New York Med. Jour.. 1890. li., 88-94.

282. Potter, H. C.: MEDICAL RECORD, New York, 1879, xv., 371.

283. Powell, J. B.: New Orleans Med. and Surg. Jour., 1855, xi., 468-470.

284. Price, J.: Amer. Jour. of Surg. and Gynec., Wellston, Mo., 1895-96, viii., 115-117.

285. Quenu : Bull. et mém. soc. de chir. de Paris, 1893, n. s., xix , 678-680.

286. Reclus, P.: Bull. et mém. soc. de chir. de Paris, 1892, n. s., xviii., 125-132.

287. Ribbert: Arch. f. path. Anat. (etc.), Berlin, 1893, cxxxii., 66-90.

288. Richardson, M. H. : Boston Med. and Surg. Jour., 1892, cxxvi , 261-263 ; cxxvii., 105-111.

289 Richardson, M. H.: Amer. Jour. of Med. Sci., Philadelphia, 1894, n. s., cvii., 1-25.

290. Richelot, L G : Bull. et mém. soc. de chir. de Paris, 1890, n. s , xvi., 625-630.

291. Richelot, L. G.: Bull. méd.. Paris, 1897, xii., 441-443.

292. Rioblanc : Gaz. des hôp., Paris, 1897, lxx., 1235.

293. Robb, H.: Johns Hopkins Hosp. Bull., Baltimore, 1892, iii., 23-25.

294. Robinson, B.: MEDICAL RECORD, New York, 1895, xlviii., 757–762.

295. Robinson, B.: MEDICAL RECORD, New York, 1895, xlviii., 373.

296. Robson, M.: British Med. Jour., London, 1896, ii., 1761–1763.

297. Rochester, T.: Buffalo Med. and Surg. Jour., 1878, xviii., 124.

298. Roger, H., et Josué, O.: Rev. de méd., Paris, 1896, xvi., 433–457.

299. Rokitansky, C.: Med. Jahrb., Wien, 1867, xiii., 179–183.

300. Rolleston, H. D.: Edinburgh Med. Jour., 1898, n. s., iv., 21–26.

301. Rosenthal, A.: MEDICAL RECORD, New York, 1898, liii., 359.

302. Rosenstirn, J.: Arch. prov. de chir., Paris, 1898, vii., 643–670.

303. Rotter, J.: Ueber Perityphlitis, Berlin, 1896, S. Karger, 8vo, 103 pages, 3 plates.

304. Roussel, A.: Loire méd., St. Etienne, 1897, xvi., 114.

305. Routier: Bull. et mém. soc. de chir. de Paris, 1896, n. s., xxii., 435, 744–747.

306. Ruth, C. E.: Mathews' Med. Quarterly, Louisville, 1895, ii., 234–236.

307. Sachs, W.: Arch. f. klin. Chir., 1895, l., 16–74.

308. Sands, H. B.: Ann. Anat. and Surg. Soc., Brooklyn, N. Y., 18°0, ii., 249–270.

309. Sands, H. B.: New York Med. Jour., 1888, xlvii., 197–205, 607.

310. Scheibenzuber, A.: Ohio Med. and Surg. Jour., Columbus, 1877, n. s., ii., 259.

311. Schooler, E.: Trans. Iowa Med. Soc., Dubuque, 1886–89, vii., 300–304.

312. Schlafke: Münchner med. Wochenschr., 1895, xlii., 752–776.

313. Schueller, M.: Arch. f. klin. Chir., Berlin, 1889, xxxix., 845–859.

314. Scott, N. S.: Trans. Ohio Med. Soc., Cleveland, 1898, 153–162.

315. Senn, N.: Jour. Amer. Med. Assoc., Chicago, 1889, xiii., 630–636.

316. Senn, M.: Jour. Amer. Med. Assoc., Chicago, 1894, xxii., 403–411.

317. Sheen, A.: Practitioner, London, 1896, lvi., 607–611.

318. Sheffey, L. B.: South. Med. and Surg. Jour., Augusta, Ga., 1849, n. s., v., 654.

319. Shiels, G. F. : Occidental Med. Times, Sacramento, 1896, x., 592-595.

320. Shoemaker. G. E.: Annals of Surgery, Philadelphia, 1898, xxvii., 7:3-740.

321. Shoemaker, G. E. : Trans. College of Physicians, Philadelphia, 1892, 3 s., xiv., 214-216.

322. Shrady, G. F.: MEDICAL RECORD, New York, 1894, xlv., 1-4

323. Simons, M. H.: Report of Surg.-Gen. of the Navy, Washington, 1896, 204.

324. Skoda: Allg. Wien. med. Zeitg., 1862, vii., 445-451.

325. Smith, S. H.: Western Lancet, Cincinnati, 1848, vii., 134-142.

326. Smith, J.: Edinburgh Med. Jour., 1895-96, xli , 402-413. 1 plate.

327. Sonnenburg: Deutsche Zeitschr. f. Chir., Leipzig, 1893-94, xxxviii , 155-295.

328. Sonnenburg, E.: Verhandl d. deutsch. Gesellsch. f. Chir , Berlin, 1896. xxv., pt. ii., 42-67.

329. Sonnenburg, E.: Pathologie u. Therapie d. Perityphlitis. 3 Aufl., Leipzig, 1897, F. C. Vogel, 8vo, 395 pages, 6 plates.

330. Sonnenburg, E.: Mitt. a. d. Grenzgeb. d. Med. u. Chir., Jena, 1898, iii , 1-21.

331. Sourdille, G.: Bull. soc. anat. de Paris, 1894, lxix., 447-451.

332. Ssawostjanow, A. I.: Med. Obozr., Moscow, 1893, xxxix., 938-943.

333. Stedman, O.: Lancet, London, 1893, i., 1061.

334. Stiegele : Med. Cor.-Bl. d. württ. ärztl. Ver., 1870, xl., 203

335. Stimson, L. A.: New York Med. Jour., 1890, lii., 449-456.

336. Stimson, L. A.: Annals of Surgery, Philadelphia, 1896, xxiii , 186.

337. Stimson, L. A.: Trans. Med. Soc., New York, Philadelphia, 1891, 235-245.

338. Sutherland, G. A : Lancet, London, 1895, ii., 457-459.

339. Swan, J. M.: Univ. Med. Mag., Philadelphia, 1895-96, viii., 194-196.

340. Symonds, C. J.: Trans. Clin. Soc. of London, 1884-85, xviii., 285-291.

341. Tait, L.: British Med. Jour., 1889, ii., 763.

342. Talamon, C.: Appendicite et perityphlite, 12mo, Paris, 1892. Translated by E. P. Hurd, 16mo, Detroit, Mich., 1893.

343. Thacher, T. H.: Proceedings New York Pathol. Soc. (1891), 1892, 71.

344. Toft : Dissertatio de fabricâ et functiore processus vermiformis, Groningue, 1840. p. 24

345. Traube : Deutsche Klinik, 1859, xi., 505–507.

346. Treves, F., and Swallow, J. D.: Lancet, London, 1889, i.,
267-269.

347. Tuffier : Semaine médicale, Paris, 1894, xiv., 5£7.

347 bis. Vanderveer, A.: Medical Review of Reviews, 1899,
v., 672.

348. Vimont : Bull. soc. anat. de Paris, 1887, lxii., 608.

349. Vineberg, H. N.: Charlotts (N. C.) Med. Jour., 1895,
vii., 17–26.

350. Vischer, C. V.: Annals of Surgery, Philadelphia, 1897,
xxvi., 624.

351. Vols, A : Die durch Kothsteine bedingte Durchbohrung
des Wurmfortsatzes die häufige verkannte Ursache einer
gefährlichen Peritonitis, und deren Behandlung mit Opium.
8vo, Carlsruhe. 1846.

352. Von Hochstetter, A. F.: Colica processus vermiformis
(Breuer) Beitr. z. Chir. Festschr. Theodor Billroth, Stuttgart,
1892. 138–143.

353. Von Mayer, Ch.: Rev. méd. de la Suisse rom., Genève,
1897, xvii., 209–255. 1 plate.

354. Von Mayer, Ch.: Rev. méd. de la Suisse rom., Genève,
1898, xviii., 285-299.

355. Vosse, J : De intestino cæco ejusque appendice vermi-
formi, sm. 4to, Gœttingæ. 1749.

356. Wallis, C.: Hygiea, Stockholm, 1892, liv., 578–595.

357. Waterhouse, H. F.: British Med. Jour., London, 1897,
ii., 1505

358. Weber, I..: Bull New York Acad. of Med., 1871, iv., 83.

359. Weeks, S. H.: Trans. Amer. Surg. Assoc., Philadelphia,
1892, x., 179-182.

360. Weir, R. F.: MEDICAL RECORD, New York, 1893, xliv.,
348.

361. Weir, R. F.: MEDICAL RECORD, New York, 1889,
xxxv., 449.

362. Weiss et Février: Rev. de chir., Paris, 1898, xviii., 596,
1166.

363. Whitall, S.: MEDICAL RECORD, New York, 1874, ix.,
255–257.

364. Wiggin, F. H.: MEDICAL RECORD, New York, 1892,
xli., 109

365. Wiliiams, H.: Medical News, Philadelphia, 1895, lxvi.,
483–480.

366. With, C. E.: Peritonitis appendicularis. Festskr. d.
Laegevidensk. Fak. v. Kjobenh. Univ., Kjobenh., 1879, No. 5,
1–84.

367. With, C. E.: Peritonitis appendicularis, etc., Kjobenh., 1897, 8vo.

368. With, C.: Congr. périod. intern. des sc. méd., compt. rend., 1884, Copenh., 1886, ii., Sect. de méd., 133–141.

369. Wolf, H. J.: New York mediz. Monatschr., 1899, xi., 275.

370. Worcester, A.: Boston Med. and Surg. Jour., 1891, cxxv., 84.

371. Wright, G. A., and Renshaw, K.: British Med. Jour., London, 1897, i., 1470.

372. Wright, J. H.: Boston Med. and Surg. Jour., 1898, cxxxviii., 150.

373. Wyeth, J. A.: New York Polyclinic, 1893, i., 63–70.

374. Wyeth, J. A.: Jour. Amer. Med. Assoc., Chicago, 1894, xxiii., 928.

375. Zdekauer, A.: Prag. med. Wochenschr., 1890, xv., 340.

376. Zuckerkandl, E.: Anat. Hefte, Wiesb., 1894, iv., 99–124, 4 plates.

59 West Forty-Ninth Street.